Kids, sometimes you forget how amazing you are.
This is your reminder.

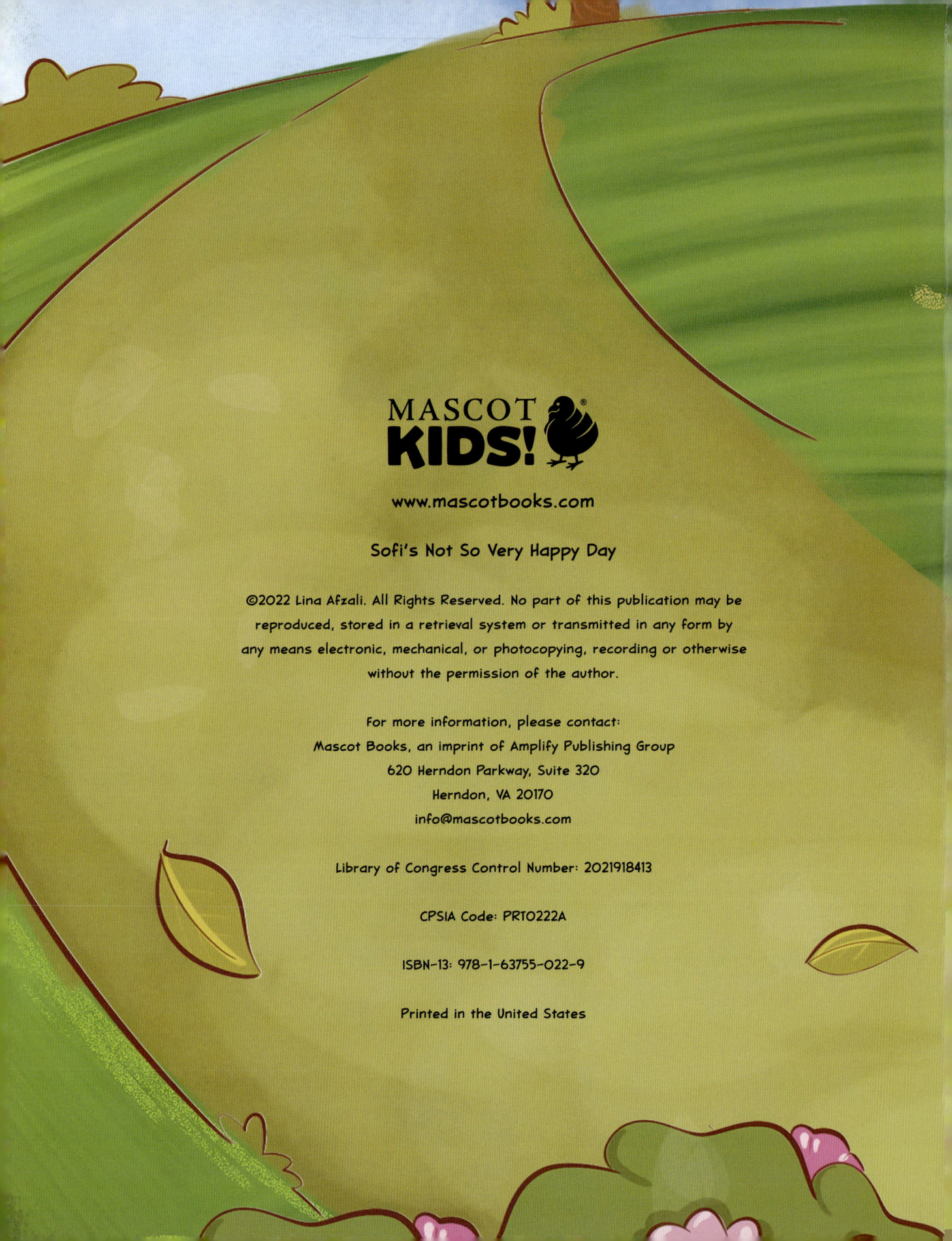

Sofi's Not So Very Happy Day

©2022 Lina Afzali. All Rights Reserved. No part of this publication may be reproduced, stored in a retrieval system or transmitted in any form by any means electronic, mechanical, or photocopying, recording or otherwise without the permission of the author.

For more information, please contact:
Mascot Books, an imprint of Amplify Publishing Group
620 Herndon Parkway, Suite 320
Herndon, VA 20170
info@mascotbooks.com

Library of Congress Control Number: 2021918413

CPSIA Code: PRT0222A

ISBN-13: 978-1-63755-022-9

Printed in the United States

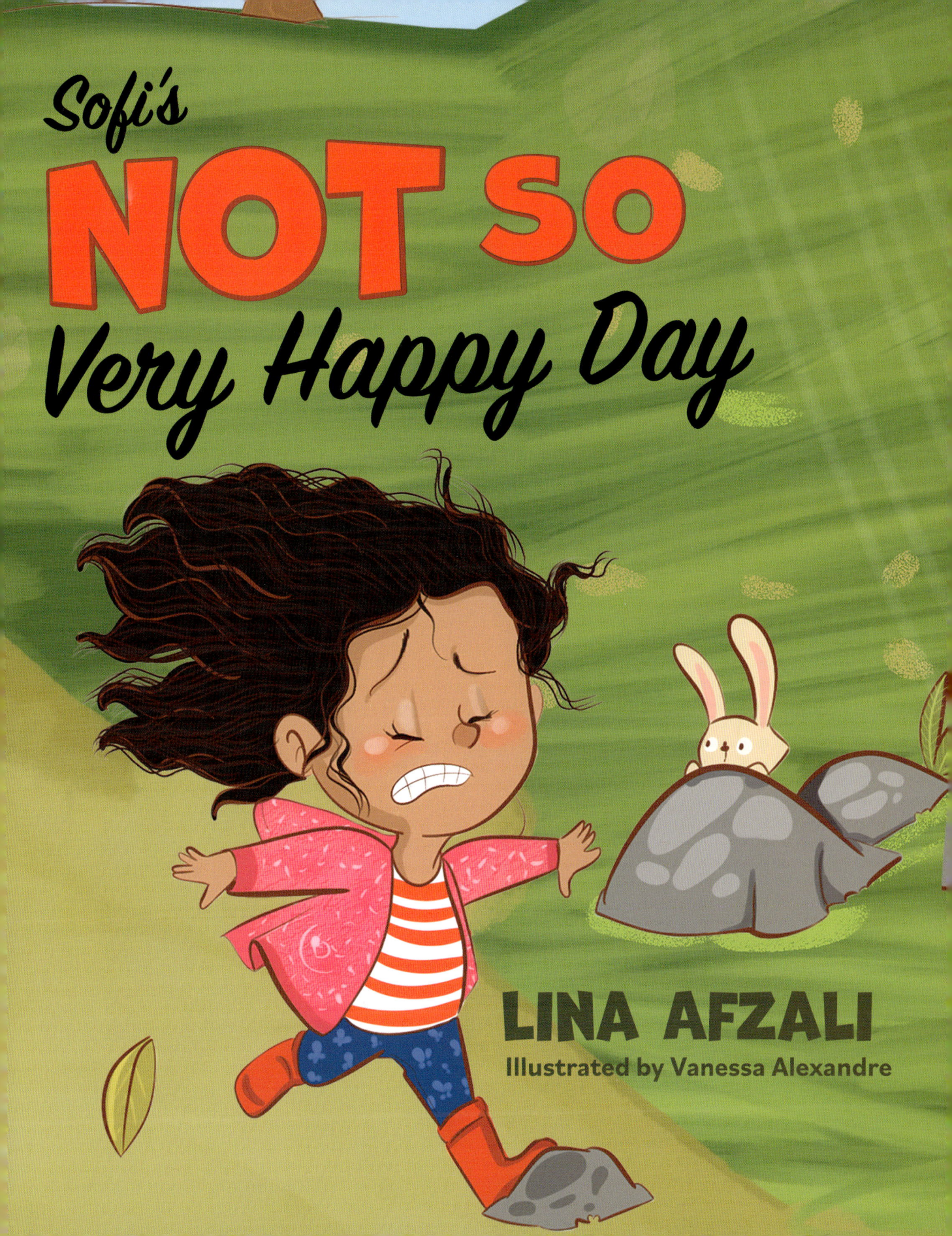

SOFI'S day started bad. As soon as she woke up, she fell out of bed and hit her head.

"OUCH!" yelled Sofi as she got to her feet. "This is **NOT** a good way to start my day."

After waking up in a terrible way, Sofi's dad thought a nice breakfast would make her feel better. He made her eggs, bacon, **AND** pancakes. Sofi's breakfast looked and smelled delicious.

I'M SO HAPPY TO BE AT DAD'S HOUSE THIS WEEK, Sofi thought. She had missed him terribly.

As she was walking to the table, she dropped her plate and her breakfast fell on the floor.

That made Sofi upset. **"BREAKFAST IS RUINED!"** Sofi wailed. "This day just keeps getting worse."

Sofi's dad decided to take her on a walk in the park. That **ALWAYS** cheered her up.

As they were strolling along, Sofi stubbed her toe on a large rock. It hurt so bad that she started to cry.

Then, it suddenly started to rain on poor Sofi's head.

Sofi and her dad ran into an ice cream shop to get out of the rain. They had so many flavors; it was making her mouth water. **ICE CREAM ALWAYS MAKES THINGS BETTER,** she thought.

Her dad ordered her a double scoop of rainbow sherbet, Sofi's favorite, but the shop had just run out. Sofi crossed her arms and declared, "No rainbow sherbet? This does not make my day any better."

After the rain stopped, Sofi and her dad stopped by their favorite restaurant for dinner. The yummy smells from inside made her tummy rumble.

When they walked in, the place was so crowded she had to wait a very long time for her food.

When the waiter finally brought Sofi her spaghetti and meatballs, the meatballs rolled off the plate and bounced away.

"**YUCK!**" Sofi exclaimed, her tummy still rumbling. "This is **NOT** turning out to be such a great day."

Sofi wanted to go home. She was having such a bad day that she just wanted to take a nice bubble bath with her favorite toys.

. . . but when Sofi and her dad finally got back home, she remembered that she had forgotten her favorite bath toys at her mom's house.

"I was so excited for my bath!" Sofi pouted. "Without my favorite toys, it won't make me feel any better."

After a disappointing bath, Sofi dressed in her PJs and sat in front of the TV with her dad.

She was hoping to watch her favorite movie, but when her dad tried to turn the TV on, it wouldn't work. Every channel was showing nothing but static. She turned the TV off and decided to go to bed instead.

"Now I can't even watch my favorite movie to cheer me up," said Sofi. "This has **NOT** been a good day."

As Sofi got into her warm, comfy bed and closed her eyes, she thought about all the things that had made her happy that day, even though things hadn't gone her way.

Even though Sofi hadn't been able to watch her favorite movie, her dad had read her their favorite bedtime story after tucking her in. **THAT WAS A GREAT WAY TO END MY DAY,** Sofi thought.

WHEN I LOST MY MEATBALLS, Sofi thought, **DAD GAVE ME HIS MEATBALLS INSTEAD. THAT CHEERED ME UP.**

She thought some more.

When she went to the ice cream shop, even though they didn't have her favorite flavor, they did have other flavors that she liked.

She had taken a walk in the park, and when it started to rain, her dad had laughed his great big belly laugh, which always made her smile.

She was even able to have her favorite breakfast with her dad, who made her more eggs, bacon, and pancakes after she dropped her plate.

Sofi also thought about how, even though her parents didn't live together, they both loved her the most.

That's what made her the happiest.

TODAY WAS ACTUALLY A PRETTY GOOD DAY, Sofi thought as she drifted off to sleep. **AND TOMORROW IS GOING TO BE EVEN BETTER!**

ABOUT THE AUTHOR

In a world filled with negativity and pain, there is also love and laughter. This idea, that there is much to be grateful for in life no matter the situation, inspired Lina Afzali to write *Sofi's Not So Very Happy Day*. As Lina has gone through her own spiritual journey, she has learned, and is still learning, to appreciate and enjoy the little things in life and to smile often. Lina believes the key to happiness is in our own minds.